MAZY ★ the MOVIE STAR

ISLA FISHER

Illustrated by PAULA BOWLES

WELBECK FLAME

*This book is dedicated to Olive, Elula, Monty
and Sacha Barking Cohen.*
I. F.

For Sushi, my favourite little sausage x
P. B.

First published in 2022 by Welbeck Flame
This paperback edition was first published in 2023 by Welbeck Flame
An imprint of Welbeck Children's Limited,
Part of the Welbeck Publishing Group

Offices in: London – 20 Mortimer Street, London W1T 3JW &
Sydney – 205 Commonwealth Street, Surry Hills 2010

www.welbeckpublishing.com

Design and layout © Welbeck Children's Limited

Text © 2022 Isla Fisher
Illustrations © 2022 Paula Bowles

A CIP catalogue record for this book is available from the British Library.

ISBN 978 1 80130 076 6

Printed in Heshan, China

10 9 8 7 6 5 4 3 2 1

Once upon a time there was a famous movie star named Mazy.

Mazy was a pampered pooch who had her fur fluffed twice a day
and her paw-nails painted pink.

While other dogs chased sticks, Mazy chased her acting dreams.

One day Mazy's acting agent delivered bad news.
"Mazy," she yapped. "The movie makers only want street dogs now.

There is no work for you any more."

Mazy was not giving up that easily.
On Monday she tried out as the lead in *Puppies of the Caribbean*.

The director sniffed. "Pirates are fierce,
not fluffy and coddled."

The door slammed shut.

On Wednesday Mazy went for an audition for *Mary Puppins*.
The film maker shook his head.

"Mary Puppins isn't petted and pandered to."

On Friday she met with the producer of *101 Dalmatians*.

"You aren't growly enough for a part in this movie!"
Mazy's tail slid between her legs.

Nobody wanted Mazy to star in their movies.

Without work, Mazy had to give up her glitzy life.

She had one last journey home in the limo, woofed goodbye to her staff and moved out of her movie-star mansion and into the dog-house.

Now there was no one to fluff Mazy's fur, or scoop her poop!

Mazy felt very, very sad.

Then she heard barking from the kennel next door. Her neighbours Buster, Patch and Gums wagged their tails. "Do you want to come to the park?"

Mazy cowered behind them.
She had never played outside without a doggy-guard.

She had never chased a ball . . .

or rolled in a muddy puddle . . .

And she had certainly NEVER peed on a bush!

This was a whole new world for Mazy!
After watching for a while, Mazy daintily followed Patch onto the grass.

Soon Mazy got braver and braver.
She leaped and lounged, sniffed and stretched.

She chased the other dogs around and laughed when they chased her back.

Mazy was so happy she didn't mind that her fur was covered in mud and her chin was all drooly.
She even joined in the tug-of-war without worrying about staining her pearly-whitened teeth.

They stopped for ice cream and Buster asked Mazy
why she wasn't making movies any more.

"I couldn't get any parts," Mazy yelped sadly.
"Film makers only want street dogs now . . ."

"But you are a street dog," Buster barked.

"You can chase a ball and play tug-of-war and roll in muddy puddles.
You could act in any movie."

Mazy felt her confidence returning.

That night, there was an audition for a movie called *Star Paws*.

Mazy ran and jumped, growled and chased.
She was her NEW self!

The director wagged his tail. "You've got the job."

Mazy barked.
"So I'm not too fluffy and friendly, petted and pandered to?"
"No, you're an every-dog, you can do everything."

Mazy loved acting in her new movie. The film *Star Paws* was a smash hit and Mazy won a Golden Bowl for her role as Chewbarka.

But she didn't go back to her old life of luxury.
You can see her at the park with her new friends,
and sometimes if no one's looking . . .

HOLLYWOOFLAND

Magic Castle

. . . you might even see her
peeing on a bush.

ISLA FISHER

Isla Fisher is a comic actress.
She has played many fun and different characters, but
her favourite role is being a mum to her three children.
She has been making up stories at bedtime
for them every night since they were born.